Hermon Griswold Batterson

Christmas Carols and Other Verses

Hermon Griswold Batterson

Christmas Carols and Other Verses

ISBN/EAN: 9783743417427

Manufactured in Europe, USA, Canada, Australia, Japa

Cover: Foto ©Andreas Hilbeck / pixelio.de

Manufactured and distributed by brebook publishing software
(www.brebook.com)

Hermon Griswold Batterson

Christmas Carols and Other Verses

CHRISTMAS CAROLS

AND

OTHER VERSES.

Christmas Carols

AND

OTHER VERSES.

BY THE

REV. H. G. BATTERSON, D.D.

PHILADELPHIA:

J. B. LIPPINCOTT & CO.

1877.

TO

MY MOTHER.

IF words of mine one soul may lead
  From ways of sin and death, to find
The place where GOD that soul shall feed,
  And to His Throne with love shall bind
The weary heart, I ask no more.
  What better can I leave behind,
Than record of that blessèd store
  Of GOD's great love for human-kind?

CONTENTS.

7

CONTENTS.

CHRISTMAS CAROLS.

The Christmas-Bells.

RING on, ye joyous Christmas-Bells!
　　Ring on!　Ring on!
What tale of love your music tells!
　　Ring on!　Ring on!
　　"The Christ" is born
　　For sinful men;
　　'Tis Christmas morn,
　　Ring out again!

Ring on, ye merry Christmas-Bells!
　　Ring on!　Ring on!
What peace from out your clangor wells!
　　Ring on!　Ring on!
　　Peace comes to earth,
　　"Good-will to men;"
　　A priceless birth,
　　Ring out again!

Ring on, ye happy Christmas-Bells!
　　Ring on!　Ring on!
With holy joy the clamour swells!
　　Ring on!　Ring on!

11

Oh, happy day
For weary men ;
Oh, royal day,
Ring out again !

Ring on, ye holy Christmas-Bells !
Ring on !   Ring on !
O'er hill and dale, through wildest dells,
Ring on !   Ring on !
In triumph ring,
For holy men
All gladness bring,
Ring out again !

Ring on, ye gladsome Christmas-Bells !
Ring on !   Ring on !
'Tis " mercy mild" the sound foretells,
Ring on !   Ring on !
The " Prince of Peace"
Now pleads for men,
Nor will he cease,
Ring out again !

Ring on, ye peaceful Christmas-Bells !
Ring on !   Ring on !
Tell of the hope that in us dwells,
Ring on !   Ring on !
To JESUS now
All ranks of men
In worship bow,
Ring out again !

On the First Bright Christmas-Day.

On the first bright Christmas-Day,
In a stable, Jesus lay,
While the angels o'er the plain
Sang the glad and sweet refrain,—
    " To GOD in the highest, all glory !
    Peace to men of good-will upon earth !"
    Hark ! hark to the wonderful story,
    Heard by shepherds the night of His birth !

Sweetly sang the angels bright
On the world's first Christmas-night ;
Brightly shone the beauteous star,
Leading sages from afar.
    " To GOD in the highest," etc.

Wise men, kings, in wonder led,
To the lowly manger-bed,
Bowed in adoration there,
Bringing gifts, both rich and rare.
    " To GOD in the highest," etc.

Lo! their treasures they unfold!
Myrrh, frankincense, shining gold!
Lay them down before His Face,
By whom cometh truth and grace.
  " To GOD in the highest," etc.

Virgin-born! We worship Thee!
Low before Thee bend the knee.
Raise our thoughts and hopes above
With our Christmas songs of love!
  "To GOD in the highest, all glory!
  Peace to men of good-will upon earth!"
  Hark! hark to the wonderful story,
  Heard by shepherds the night of His birth!

Joyfully, Joyfully, Angels are Singing.

JOYFULLY, joyfully, angels are singing,
  O'er Bethlehem's plains of light!
Wonderful, wonderful message now bringing,
  To welcome the Christmas night!
    " Glory to GOD in the highest, all glory !
      Peace on the earth, and good-will :"
    Angels are telling the marvellous story,
      Shepherds are list' ning still.

Peacefully, peacefully, light is now beaming,
  Sages have come from afar;
Beautiful, beautiful, brightly now gleaming,
  Bethlehem's wonderful star!
    " Glory to GOD," etc.

Wistfully, wistfully, wise men are seeking
  " The Christ" in the " House of Bread ;"
Tenderly, tenderly, MARY is keeping
  Her watch o'er that lowly bed.
    " Glory to GOD," etc.

Lovingly, lovingly, kings now adore Him,
   And offer their humble prayer ;
Faithfully, faithfully worship before Him,
   While bringing their gifts so rare !
    " Glory to GOD," etc.

Merrily, merrily, Church-Bells are ringing
   O'er all the wide world so bright ;
Thankfully, thankfully, gifts we are bringing,
   For this is our Christmas night !
    " Glory to GOD," etc.

Joyfully, joyfully, o'er every nation
   The " banner of love" display ;
Wonderful, wonderful news of salvation,
   Our SAVIOUR is born to-day !
    " Glory to GOD in the highest, all glory !
     Peace on the earth, and good-will :"
    Angels are telling the marvellous story,
    Shepherds are list'ning still.

HYMNS.

2* 17

Hymn for Advent.

" He cometh to judge the earth."

THE last dread trump is sounding !
  Heaven's pearly gates unfold :
The Judge, with might abounding,
  Ye nations, now behold !
      Heaven is shaking,
      Earth is quaking,
Death's grim record see unrolled.

With angel-hosts surrounded ;
  On glory-clouds His Throne !
Hell's legions now confounded,
  Must yield the King His own.
      Sinners moaning,
      Crimes now owning,
Which before were all unknown !

In piteous tones now pleading,
  In terror and in fear ;
All other cries unheeding
  Save this one, " Saviour, hear !"

19

Man is sighing,
Bitter crying !—
See at last the Judge appear.

Let faithful souls, victorious,
  With joy and gladness sing ;
While heavenly hosts all glorious,
  On light and joyous wing,
    With the story
    Of His glory
Make the starry arches ring !

With shouts of rapt devotion
  And songs of holy joy,
From ocean back to ocean,
  Ye saints, your tongues employ ;
    Filled with gladness,
    Past all sadness,
Peace He brings without alloy !

Epiphany.

"We have seen His star in the east."

THE STAR OF BETHLEHEM

STAR of morning! Star of evening!
　Star of life's most dismal day:
Star of all the stars the brightest,
　Star that guides our devious way.

Heavenly star! with joyous wonder
　Sages watched thy path of light;
And the shepherds with the angels,
　Saw the heavens with thee bedight.

Star of Bethl'em, star of wonder!
　Star of Jacob, leading now;
Touch our souls with adoration
　As before "The Christ" we bow.

Oh, how bright thy glorious shining!
　Oh, how full of peace thy light!
Guide us through life's darkest danger
　With thy rays of hope so bright.

Star of morning! star of evening!
　Star of love, now lead us on,
With the shepherds and the Wise men
　JESU'S FACE to gaze upon.

Lent.

"If we confess our sins, He is faithful and just to forgive us our sins."

SAVIOUR, now before Thee bending,
While our prayers and tears are blending,
Hear our cries to heaven ascending :
    Now adoring,
    Now imploring,
    O deliver us, GOOD LORD !

By Thy Cross we kneel, bemoaning,
All our sins before Thee owning,
And we plead Thy Blood atoning,
    In confession
    For transgression :
    O deliver us, GOOD LORD !

See us in our sad condition,
Bowed in deep and true contrition ;
Hear our pleading, strong petition,
    One Foundation,
    One Salvation,
    O deliver us, GOOD LORD !

Satan's toils long years have bound us;
But Thy Mercy now has found us,
Let Thy Grace, O Lord, surround us,
　　Sin confounding,
　　Love abounding,
　　O deliver us, GOOD LORD!

Lord, we plead "Thy Cross and Passion,"
Boundless love, and deep compassion,
Godhead, clothed in human fashion,
　　On high reigning,
　　All sustaining,
　　O deliver us, GOOD LORD!

"Thine the Name that brings salvation;"
Come and rule o'er every nation,
Claim by right all adoration;
　　For our yearning,
　　Love returning,
　　O deliver us, GOOD LORD!

Hymn for Good-Friday.

"Lord, remember me when Thou comest into Thy Kingdom."

O JESU LORD! now crucified,
With arms of love extended wide,
I pray Thee, by Thy wounded side,
    O Lord, remember me!

O JESU LORD! in hope and fear,
To Thy dread cross I now draw near,
And plead Thy love to man so dear;—
    O Lord, remember me!

O JESU LORD! with deep amaze
As on Thy woeful grief I gaze,
My earnest cry to Thee I raise;—
    O Lord, remember me!

O JESU LORD! Thy bitter woe
I ne'er can feel, nor ever know;
Yet from Thy cross one word bestow;—
    O Lord, remember me!

O JESU LORD! to Thee I call,
And weeping, at Thy feet I fall:
My GOD, my hope, my all in all;—
    O Lord, remember me!

O JESU LORD! so full of grace,
Look on me with Thy loving Face;
Me,—in Thy kingdom grant a place;—
    O Lord, remember me!

O JESU LORD! teach me Thy will,
Help me all duty to fulfil;
Teach me to know Thee, and be still:—
    O Lord, remember me!

O JESU LORD! be Thou my peace;
Give of Thy love the full increase,
And from my sins grant Thou release;—
    O Lord, remember me!

O JESU LORD! in my last hour,
When clouds and darkness round me lour,
Come with Thy mercy, love, and power!—
    O Lord, remember me!

O JESU LORD! great King of kings!
Beneath the shadow of Thy wings
My weary heart its burden brings;—
    O Lord, remember me!

Easter.

" All her streets shall say, Alleluia."

Alleluia ! Alleluia ! Alleluia !
Alleluia ! Risen Lord !
To Thee, O Christ, victorious King of kings,
    Our Easter songs of gladness now we raise ;
O'er all the earth the joyous strain upsprings
    To hail Thee Victor on this " Queen of Days !"

Alleluia ! Lord of Life !
Death's brazen gates, unbarred for evermore,
    Are radiant now with light that comes from Thee ;
The darkness passed—we see the open door
    Through which comes Life and Immortality !

Alleluia ! Victor King !
Hail ! hail ! Thou Victor over death and hell !
    All earthly triumphs sink before Thine Own ;
All nations now with joy and rapture tell
    Of sealèd tomb, changed to a glorious Throne !

Alleluia ! Prince of Peace !
Oh, happy day ! thrice welcome to our hearts,
    Long bound with sin and shame before Thy cross :
Oh, glorious day ! which to the world imparts
    That gift, before which all our wealth is dross !

26

Alleluia! Evermore!
Hail! "Lion of the tribe of Judah!" hail!
What gift is this Thy nail-pierced hands do bring?
Eternal Life! a life that cannot fail:
All glory to Thy Name, O mighty King!

Ascension.

" God is gone up, with a merry noise."

LIFT up your heads, ye pearly gates,
Throw open wide heaven's guarded doors ;
For He who triumphed over hell
His glory and His grace outpours.

Give way ! give way ! the Conqueror comes !
With palm of vict'ry in His hands :
Greet Him with shouts of holy joy,
Ye heavenly choirs and angel bands.

The King of Peace with glory comes,
Triumphant o'er the powers of hell ;
Lift up your heads, ye glist'ning gates,
Ye hosts of heaven, His wonders tell !

Bright Cherubim in glad array,
And Seraphim, a countless band,
Lead to the Throne our risen King,
The eternal Throne at GOD's Right Hand.

To Thee, in gladsome songs of love,
We lift our hymns of thankful praise,
O Christ, Redeemer, Saviour, GOD,
In endless strains, to endless days !

28

Whitsun-tide.

"Now there are diversities of gifts, but the same Spirit."

COME, Holy Spirit ! with Thy wondrous treasures !
   Come, fill our souls with holy light ;
Thy gifts outpour, with love that never measures
   Aught but our needs, in earth's dark night.

Wisdom ! we seek Thee now, with ardent longing ;
   As pilgrims in their journey crave
The springs of water, in the desert flowing,
   In which their weary limbs to lave.

That we may have the power of *Understanding*
   The love of GOD for sinful men :
This grace, O give us, and without demanding
   More than our love to Thee again.

The gift of *Counsel*, now on us bestowing
   In mercy to our darkened souls ;
To guide us when the billows are o'erflowing,
   And Jordan's stormy water rolls.

Thy *Ghostly Strength* be with us now, abiding
  To aid in warfare with the foe
That lurks about our pathway, hiding ;
  Yet luring on to endless woe.

The gift of *Knowledge* be Thou ever giving,
  To lift our hearts from earth to Thee ;
That we, while here, by godly living,
  From godless joys may learn to flee.

True Godliness, with life to us eternal,
  Protecting here, from pit and snare,
So surely set by demon hosts infernal,
  As we to heaven our way would fare.

Give *Holy Fear !* Thy last, best gift outpouring,
  O Spirit of the GOD of Might !
While we Thy mercy and Thy love adoring,
  Will worship Thee, O GOD of Light !

Hymn to the Trinity.

"There are three that bear record in heaven."

ALLELUIA to the Father,
Lord of all the worlds above;
GOD, our Guide in every danger,
GOD of Gods and GOD of Love.
      Alleluia ! Alleluia !
      Alleluia to our God !

Alleluia ! sing to Jesus,
Praises sing to God the Son :
Jesus, King, Redeemer, Saviour,
Sing the triumph He has won !
      Alleluia ! Alleluia !
      Alleluia to our King !

Alleluia to the Spirit,
Sent of God, through Christ the Son ;
Alleluia sing we ever,
For the Comforter is come !
      Alleluia ! Alleluia !
      Alleluia to our Lord !

31

Alleluia! praise and glory
Sing we to the Triune God:
Praise the Lord, ye earth-born children,
Sing ye to our fathers' God!
    Alleluia! Alleluia!
    All ye nations praise the Lord!

Adoration.

" Blessed is He that cometh in the Name of the Lord."

JESU ! our Lord and GOD !
   We bend the knee to Thee :
Adoring, low we bow,
   In faith, Thy Presence see.

JESU ! our Lord and GOD !
   As suppliants, here we plead
For pardon, grace, and strength ;
   Oh, hear us in our need !

JESU ! our Lord and GOD !
   Hear now our earnest prayer ;
Oh, take our sins away !
   Give us Thy love and care.

JESU ! our Lord and GOD !
   Help Thou our fight with sin,
Keep Thou our footsteps here,
   Wash Thou our souls within.

Jesu ! our Lord and God !
   Adoring, low we fall ;
All hail !   Thou " Wonderful !"
   Our God, our all in all !

Jesu ! our Lord and God !
   Our star in earth's dark night,
Guide Thou our journey through,
   And then—Oh, give us light !

Jesu ! our Lord and God !
   Accept our humble prayer ;
Watch o'er our wanderings here,
   That we may know Thee there !

Saint John Baptist.

"The voice of one crying in the wilderness."

Hark ! a voice from out the desert
   Crying to the sons of men ;
"Lo, He cometh !   Lo, He cometh !"
   Now it cries, with Prophet's ken.

"This is He for whom the nations
   Waited long in hope to see ;
Now He cometh, clothed with meekness,
   To His standard, sinners, flee !"

By fair Jordan's holy waters
   Lo, the Baptist sternly stands ;
Now the kingdom quickly cometh,
   Will ye meet its loud demands ?

Cast aside your vain oblation,
   Works bring forth for penance meet ;
Bow before Him, weary-hearted,
   Cast your idols at His feet.

33

This is He, Who cometh after,
    Yet preferred before shall be ;
He, the latchet of Whose sandals
    None are worthy to set free.

He in Whom both truth and mercy
    Linked together now for aye ;
Come with blessings for the weary,
    Countless blessings day by day.

Sent from GOD, this blessèd message
    Beareth he of MARY'S SON ;
Crying in Judea's wildness,
    As before Him he doth run :

"Lo, He cometh !   Lo, He cometh !
    He of Whom the Prophets told ;
He to Whom the waiting nations
    Turned their hopes in days of old !"

"Theotokos."

"MOTHER of God !" Oh, blessèd name !
Through all the ages still the same ;
Let men on earth, with holy love,
Join in the strain, now sung above.

" Blessèd art thou !" yea, blessèd still,
Obedient to GOD's holy will ;
Though Queen of all the saints in light,
And Virgin pure, with grace bedight.

Hail, Mary ! Mother of our GOD !
Still " handmaid" in the blest abode
Of perfect spirits, men made just,
Prophets and Martyrs, men who trust

For final bliss to thy dear SON,
Who by His Blood for them has won
Eternal rest—perpetual light—
And triumphed over sin's dark night.

Mother of GOD! we yield to thee
As to the Cross we fain would flee;
"All but adoring love," and own
As our Redeemer—MARY'S SON.

Ora pro nobis, Mother dear,
As o'er the earth we walk in fear,
Pray sin may in us conquered be,
That we at last may rest with thee!

Saint Augustine.

"Such honor have all His saints."

SAINT AUGUSTINE! marching onward,
    With the Cross uplifted high;
See! the heathen King to greet thee
    Waits with Queen and nobles nigh:
March then forward, nothing fearing,
    Lift thy banner to the sky!

Saint Augustine! Christ's Evangel!
    Great the trust GOD gives to thee;
Wondrous message thou art bringing
    To the "Islands of the Sea;"
Message fraught with greatest blessings
    Now, and for eternity!

Saint Augustine! lift the Standard!
    Wave thy banner! know no fear!
Christ's Commission now thou bearest,
    Whether men forbear or hear;
And the word thou this day speakest
    Must be bold, and strong and clear.

Saint Augustine ! England's Angel !
   Speak for Christ thy Master now !
Tell the story of Redemption
   Wrought for men on Calvary's brow ;
Speak the word with gentle boldness,
   And the King to Christ shall bow.

Saint Augustine ! Holy Warrior !
   Thou hast fought thy battle well !
Lo ! the King as " nursing Father !"
   Let the Church the story tell !
And the Queen a " nursing Mother,"
   As the Prophet did foretell !

Saint Augustine ! Blessed Bishop !
   Fold thine arms and lay thee down ;
Rest—eternal rest—thy portion,
   Thy reward—the Victor's Crown !
Light—perpetual light—thy glory,
   Crown uplifted—Cross laid down !

England ! England ! now and ever
   Cherish God's great gift to thee :
Tell thy children of Augustine ;
   And their children, yet to be,
Shall the great Confessor honor
   In these " Islands of the Sea !"

Penitence.

O JESU! at Thy blessèd Feet
  I lay my sinful, weary heart ;
This holy refuge, my retreat,
  From which I fain would ne'er depart.

With throbbing heart and trembling frame
  I bow before Thee, Saviour—God :—
Touched with a sense of guilt and shame,
  I bow me down to kiss Thy rod !

O JESU! Brother, Friend, and Guide !
  Plead for me at the Father's Throne ;
Hide Thou within Thy Wounded Side
  The sins for which Thou didst atone.

The mem'ry of Thy dripping Cross,
  With outstretched arms Thy love to give,
Comes to my soul in its dread loss
  And bids me look to Thee and live !

Ah me ! and must I bear this load,
  This burden great of countless sins:
And must I tread the weary road,
  Where guilt mine ear forever dins ?

I think of my rebellious will,
  A grievous, weary, woeful thought ;
My heart is faint ;—mine eyes now fill
  With tears, for life has been for naught.

Oh, hide me with Thy Cross of love,
  Pardon and cleanse my sinful soul ;
Give me at last a place above,
  Where songs of praise forever roll !

The Name of Jesus.

"At the Name of Jesus every knee shall bow."

WE kneel to Thee, our dearest Saviour !
 For we need Thy watchful care ;
We need Thy love and Thy protection,
 To help us here our cross to bear.

We kneel to Thee, our dearest Saviour !
 None else can save us, Lord, but Thee ;
Thine earthly mission was to sinners,
 And such we own ourselves to be.

We kneel to Thee, our dearest Saviour !
 'Tis Thy great love that bids us come ;
Oh, speak to us the words of comfort
 That gave the sinning thief a home !

We kneel to Thee, our dearest Saviour !
 Sin brings us to Thee in our need :
Oh, loving Shepherd of the outcast,
 Hear now as we for pardon plead !

We kneel to Thee, our dearest Saviour!
  Nor wait we for another call;
For Thou hast bid us come when weary,
  And offer'd pardon, free to all.

We kneel to Thee, our dearest Saviour!
  Naught but Thy grace can save us now;
Oh, Saviour! hear our earnest pleading,
  Hear, as before Thy cross we bow.

We kneel to Thee, our dearest Saviour!
  Oh, hear us, pity, and forgive;
Look on us with Thine eyes of mercy,
  And bid us look to Thee and live!

Light of the World.

"Jesus said, I am the Light of the world."

LIGHT of the world! out of the deep we call!
  Oh, hear our supplicating voice
From out the deep, where darkness doth appall
  The heart, that fears naught else but Thee.

Light of the world! in pity hear our cry;
  Be not extreme, O Lord, but hide
What we have done amiss in life's dark way;
  For we Thy wrath can ne'er abide.

Light of the world! mercy is found with Thee!
  For this we walk in holy fear;
Though darkness cover, and the gloom surround,
  We wait Thy light, our hearts to cheer.

Light of the world! we look to Thee in hope;
  We wait in faith and holy dread;
Trusting in Thee, whose word can never fail;
  Oh, hear us, lift us from the dead.

45

Light of the world ! the morning watch doth call
   Our souls in love and hope to Thee :
Thy light, like day-spring rising in our hearts,
   From sin and death can set us free.

Light of the world ! in Thee lay Israel's trust,
   Redemption from his sin to find ;
But mercy mild, with healing in his wings.
   Comes from Thy light, to all mankind.

Hymn for a Mission.

"Ho, every one that thirsteth, come ye to the waters."

Come, drink at the fountain of love and of peace,
  Ye weary, wan travellers, come!
Come, taste the sweet waters of mercy and grace,
  That flow from our Heavenly home!

'Tis Jesus now bids you,—oh, come at His call,
  Though weary and worn you may be;
His pity and bounty extend to you all,
  Oh, come! that His love you may see.

The merciful Saviour, Who died on the Cross,
  With outstretching arms to the world,
There opened the fountain that flows without loss,
  And His banner of love unfurled.

Come, lay down the burden of sin and of woe,
  Though red and like crimson it be;
The Saviour will cleanse it, and whiter than snow;
  His pity will bid you go free.

47

Oh, let not His sorrows for you be in vain !
  Do not His great bounty abuse !
He poured out His blood that your souls He might
    gain ;
  How can you such mercy refuse ?

Ho ! come to the waters ! the waters so free !
  Come all that by sin are oppressed !
The crucified Saviour cries, " Come now to Me,"
  " Ye weary ones, come to My rest !"

Ho ! come to the waters ! the waters of light !
  Both Spirit and Bride bid you come ;
Come, all who are burdened with sin's weary blight,
  Come, come to your Heavenly home !

Ho ! come to the waters ! the waters of life !
  Come, buy without money or price !
Who drinks at this fountain shall know no more strife
  With sin's blackened armor of vice.

Come, drink at the fountain of love and of peace,
  Ye weary, wan travellers, come !
Come, taste the sweet waters of mercy and grace,
  That flow from our Heavenly home !

Forgiveness.

O JESU ! Thou the wrath of man
  His hate and fury tasted :
While his salvation Thou didst plan
  He to destruction hasted.
     Thy Hands he bound,
     Thy Head he crowned,
  Thy Precious Blood he wasted.

The scoffing crowd before Thee stood,
  The ribald throng was jesting ;
While hanging on the cursèd wood,
  The thorns Thy Brow investing,
     The dying thief,
     In all Thy grief,
  Was Thy great pity testing.

Shall I forget, O Saviour mine !
  How woe and love were blended ?
And, asking mercy such as Thine
  May be to me extended,

C   5   49

With angry heart
Refuse my part
To those who have offended ?

Forgive me, Lord, my grievous sins,
Oh, hear my earnest pleading !
And as my prayer Thy pardon wins
Let me, my duty heeding,
With grateful song
Forgive each wrong
That is forgiveness needing.

Forgive, O Lord ! each bitter word ;
And for their hate give blessing.
Let this, my prayer, in heaven be heard,
And I, my love expressing,
In songs of praise
My voice will raise,
Thy mercy great, confessing.

Hymn of the Holy Child.

SING we now the praises
  Of the Holy child ;
JESU, Son of Mary
  Ne'er by sin defiled.

In a cheerless stable,
  In a crib, a King !
Unclean beasts around Him,
  White-winged angels sing.

Mary, Blessèd Mother,
  Foldeth in her arms
Christ, the world's Redeemer,
  Safe from world's alarms.

Standing in the 'Temple,
  Wond'ring people saw
Blood in red drops flowing
  To fulfil the law.

Once amid the Doctors
  Stood the spotless youth,
And with wise disputing
  Teaching them the truth.

At the Feast in Cana
  Water turned to wine,
By the royal mandate
  Of His power Divine.

At the city's gateway
  Stood the Holy One,
Nain's sad widow cheering,
  Bidding back her son.

Deaf and blind awaiting,
  Cry with strong appeal ;
Eye and ear He toucheth,
  And that touch doth heal.

Walking on the water,
  He who rules the waves,
Bids the zealous Peter
  Come to Him who saves.

Lo ! upon the mountain
  Hungry thousands meet ;
He the scant food blesseth,
  Giving all to eat.

Little children touching
  With a fond caress ;
In His arms He holds them,
  And doth each one bless.

Jesu! Jesu! Saviour!
  Children waiting here
Seek Thy love and blessing
  With Thy holy fear.

Keep us, Lord and Master,
  Free from sin and strife;
On us love bestowing,
  Jesu! Lord of Life!

5*

Hymn for Children.

WRITTEN FOR THE SUNDAY-SCHOOL OF S. MARK'S CHURCH, PHILADELPHIA.

O JESU, LORD! Thou art the Way
  Through this dark world of sin ;
Our outward pathway day by day,
  Our light, our life within.

O JESU, LORD! Thou art the Truth,
  By which we know the Way!
In all the dangers of our youth
  Thou art our hope and stay.

O JESU, LORD! Thou art the Life
  Of every loving heart ;
Keep us, O Lord, from sin and strife,
  To us Thy grace impart.

O JESU, LORD! In Thy dear Name,
  That source of living light,
We find love's best and brightest flame,
  Our guide for day or night.

54

O JESU, LORD! We trust in Thee,
  Eternal fount of grace!
And to Thy Cross in faith we flee,
  To find our resting-place.

FUGITIVES.

To My Mother:

ON HER SEVENTY-SIXTH BIRTHDAY.

Ah, Mother mine, how turns my heart to thee,
  As years speed onward to life's mournful end ;
How full with tears mine eyes, that now can see
  Naught else but failure, both of fame and friend.

The morning when I turned my back on thee
  To face the world, that seemed to me so bright ;
My purpose true ; my heart so full of glee ;
  I reck'd not, went before so dark a night.

How turned mine eyes for one last look of home,
  As o'er the hill I sped me, fast away ;
How little thought, with heart so like a stone,
  That thou wast turning back, for me to pray.

How bright the glory of that shining morn !
  What dreams of future conquest I had made !
Ah, well for me I knew not of the storm
  That soon would crush the vision there displayed.

59

In happy days, how thickly trooped the friends
  To greet me with their smiles and words of cheer !
How each did watchful, and with care attend
  To share my joys, and quench all thought of fear !

But trouble with its chilling blast came on,
  To sweep before it fortune, home, and fame ;
And like the morning dew, my friends were gone,
  Forgetting (yes ! it may be !) e'en my name.

How true it is,—" this life is but a dream !"
  At best, I found it but " an empty show ;"
While struggling vainly onward 'gainst the stream,
  I strove to hide with smiles my heartfelt woe.

Oh, friendship ! false and fickle,—yet how fair !
  But love there is no sorrow can assail :—
Though life may be a long and fretting care,
  A Mother's love will never, never fail.

Ah, Mother dear, what love more true than thine ?
  It knows no waning, falt'ring, nor decay ;
In darkest hours it ever has been mine,
  Beams on me now, a bright and endless day !

God bless thee, Mother mine, for thy strong love ;
  God bring thee safely to His rest at last ;
God give to thee the looked-for home above,
  When earthly duties, sorrows, all are passed !

St. Luke's Church, Germantown, Pennsylvania.

LINES SUGGESTED BY THE SERMON PREACHED
BY THE RT. REV. WM. BACON STEVENS, D.D.,
LL.D., ON THE DAY OF CONSECRATION,

June 8th, 1876.

"This is none other but the House of God, and this is the Gate of
Heaven."—GENESIS xxviii. 17.

THE very House of GOD ! It was one stone
Rough and unhewn ; but House of GOD it was,
And there GOD blessed the builder. And as tenth
Of all his increase came from year to year,
He laid it down in mem'ry of the vow
There made. So GOD did bless him more and more,
And made for him a name which standeth yet
Memorial of the deed at Bethel done,
Wherein he consecrated self to GOD,
And tithe perpetual vowed, of all that He
Should give in years to come, to him and his.

A thousand miles the river Nile flows on,
Unfed by any stream from other source
Than its own head.   Then, spreading out its arms
In loving bounty,. covers all the land
With fatness, while it feeds with gen'rous hand
The swarthy dweller on its swelling banks,
As moving onward to the briny sea.

A thousand years, and Jacob's faithful sons
Together banded, waiting for the time
In which should come the promised Shiloh.   Then,
When He, in majesty and agony
Was lifted up to draw the nations out
From sin, and death, and darkness to Himself,
The types and shadows of His glory passed ;
And, pouring forth in bright effulgent streams,
Rich blessings flowed from out the holy hill
And covered all the earth.
                              'Twas but one stone,
And yet, in very truth, it was BETH–EL.
So this bright Fane, in its proportions fair ;
Its carved and goodly stones ; its Nave and Aisle ;
Its gleaming Altar in the eastern wall,
Is Bethel too.
                    The painted windows tell
The wondrous story of His earthly life,
Who came to scatter blessings far and wide,
So long pent up in Israel's land alone.
Here to the generations yet unborn
Will stand this bless'd memorial of the faith

Of those who, in a faithless age, dared build
In thankful homage, and in love to GOD,
A house where He His Name in glory writes;
And where—as once in Jacob's time—He stoops
To bless the uplifted, consecrated stone.

"Not yours, but GOD's." 'Tis consecrated now,
And from this day let none profane its walls,
Or claim by right a privilege beyond
That one which all men have :—of kneeling here
In penitence and prayer, and so to gain
The benediction of GOD's bounteous love !

O GOD ! the GOD of Bethel ! come and bless
Each faithful soul, who from his penury,
Or from his wealth, has made a gift of love
Wherewith to build this goodly house to Thee,
And so record his faith, and by these stones
To tell in future days his trust in GOD.
      From desecration keep these holy walls,
And bid Thy guardian angels stand within,—
As erst of old, above the Mercy Seat,
With "wing-veiled face," they stood at Thy command.
Bless each and every soul who here is brought
With faith and love, and offered up to Thee.
Bless old and young :—the gray-haired and the child ;
Bring all within the circle of Thy love,
And bow each heart obedient to Thy will.
Grant, when their earthly labors all are passed,

These " gathered in" before the Great White Throne,
" Well done," may hear, and entering then
The " House not made with hands,"—a Bethel still,—
May see Thee—GOD of Glory—face to face !

𝔄 Paraphrase.

THE FORGET-ME-NOT.

THE Father gave all flowers a name,
    And each one had its own ;
But soon a wee one backward came,
    And, standing by His Throne,
With timid grace and trembling frame,
    The modest blue eyes fell ;
And then it said, almost with shame,
    " How it can be I cannot tell,
But Father dear, my name ! my name !
    Alas ! I have forgot !"
The Father kindly said,—" no blame,
    My child,—*Forget-me-not !*"

Pennsylvania.

THE PRAYER OF HER LOYAL SONS.

Sung at the opening exercises, PENNSYLVANIA DAY, at the CENTEN-
NIAL EXPOSITION, September 28, 1876.

GREAT GOD! our Father, hear;
Lend now Thy gracious ear;
  To Thee we pray:—
Give of Thy bounteous grace;
Bless of mankind.each race;
Let all Thy goodness trace,
  In life's dark way.

Great GOD! our Father, hear;
Teach us Thy Name to fear,
  In holy dread:
Make wars and strife to cease;
Oh give perpetual peace;
So earth shall yield increase
  Of "daily bread."

Great GOD! our Father, hear;
Guide all, both far and near,
  In our dear land:

In union, strength to find ;
One, both in heart and mind ;
O GOD ! Thy people bind
  In love's strong band.

Great GOD ! our Father, hear ;
While for our country dear
  We wait and pray :
Guard from invading foe ;
Keep from intestine woe ;
Some good, for " token" show ;
  Thy love display.

Great GOD ! our Father, hear ;
As suppliants we appear
  Before Thy Throne :
Let not the foot of pride
Come near us to abide ;
Be Thou our earthly guide,
  And lead us home.

Great GOD ! our Father, hear ;
Make Thou our pathway clear
  With heavenly light :
Bless Thou our beauteous land,
While we as brothers stand,
In union firm and grand,
  To guard the right !

Pleasant Words.

"Pleasant words are as an honeycomb, sweet to the soul, and health to the bones."—PROVERBS xvi. 24.

PLEASANT WORDS are full of sweetness
    To the heart oppressed with care ;
Peace they bring, and bounteous gladness,
    Light and love the garb they wear.
Treasured more by far than rubies,
    Yet, alas ! how sadly rare !

Pleasant Words come to the weary
    Like a sweet and dreamless sleep ;
Strength, and life, and health bestowing,
    As from fountains broad and deep,
Welling up in sandy deserts
    Sparkling waters onward sweep.

Pleasant Words are words of comfort,
    Messengers of trust and love,
Laden well with richest blessings
    From the treasure-house above ;

Borne on wings of hope and mercy,
 Gentle as the Holy Dove.

Pleasant Words of quiet meekness
 Scatter doubts and banish fears ;
Angry tongues may gather round us,
 Crushing hopes and causing tears ;
Words of kindness heal the anguish,
 Darkness flies, and light appears.

Pleasant Words of large compassion
 Spring from tender hearts and true ;
Strong with gladness, hope and courage,
 Ever old and ever new,
Leading souls with sorrow burdened
 Earth's dark journey safely through.

Pleasant Words are like the noonday,
 Cheering with a glad delight ;
Falsehood's breath may scorch and hurt us,
 Turning all our day to night :
Friendship's words of trustful pleading
 Cover all our paths with light !

The Vesper-Bells.

THE rosy clouds fade in the west,
  And pass away from sight,
While o'er the mountain's rugged crest
  (Sweet harbingers of night!)
The vesper-bells ring out the praise
Of Him who crowns with love the days,
  We in His Name delight.

The storm-clouds gather, dark and gray,
  As evening shades draw near;
The pealing thunder far away
  Falls trembling on the ear;
Yet still the evening bells awake
The vesper call, our prayers to make
  In love and holy fear.

The drifting snow goes flying fast
  O'er cottage and o'er hall;
The storm-tossed ships ride in the blast,
  Nor fear what may befall;
While evening bells once more we hear,
As bidding men no storm to fear,
  For God is all in all.

In cloud or sunshine, joy or woe,
　　God's love is still the same ;
His arm protects from every foe,
　　If, trusting in His Name,
At sound of ‾evening bells we haste
And bend the knee that love to taste
　　In consecrated fane.

'Tis not alone the music sweet
　　Of those dear bells we hear ;
But to those hearts attuned to meet
　　Our God, by faith so near,
They tell of glory all our own,
When we before the Great White Throne,
　　Freed from our bonds, appear.

To E. P. W.

ON HER SIXTY-SEVENTH BIRTHDAY.

My dear, kind friend! you pass to-day
Another mile-stone, grim and gray,
That points you o'er the world's highway
          To GOD.

Another year of joys and cares,
In which "our Father's" love prepares
Your soul for Him,—and still He spares
          His rod.

The busy world is rushing on,
Nor thinks nor cares for days once gone,
If only wealth it heaps, upon
          A clod.

It heeds not age, it heeds not youth,
Nor knows of love, nor cares for truth ;
It only makes of gold—forsooth!
          A God.

71

A work-day world ! its anxious face
Knows naught of mercy, nor of grace ;
But onward, in a feverish race
                    To plod.

You know it well ! its smiles, its tears,
Have followed you these weary years.
And its reward ?   What now appears ?
                    A sod.

Look onward to that shining band,
Beyond earth's false and shifting sand,
Where rest is found, in Holy Land,
                    With GOD !

THE END.